D1464690

995165541 6

This SCRIBBLERS
book belongs to:

....

For my husband, Philip, with so much love and heartfelt
thanks for all his kindness and support over the years.

ED

To my wonderful Mum and Dad x.

SR

This edition published in Great Britain in MMXXI
by Scribblers, an imprint of
The Salariya Book Company Ltd
25 Marlborough Place,
Brighton BN1 1UB
www.salariya.com

SALARIYA
SCRIBO BOOK HOUSE SCRIBBLERS

© The Salariya Book Company Ltd MMXXI
Text © Elizabeth Dale MMXXI
Illustrations © Siân Roberts MMXXI

PB ISBN-13: 978-1-913337-15-5

1 3 5 7 9 8 6 4 2

A CIP catalogue record for this book is
available from the British Library.

Printed and bound in Malta.

Printed on paper from sustainable sources.

All rights reserved. No part of this publication may be reproduced, stored
in or introduced into a retrieval system or transmitted in any form, or by
any means (electronic, mechanical, photocopying, recording or otherwise)
without the written permission of the publisher. Any person who does any
unauthorised act in relation to this publication may be liable to criminal
prosecution and civil claims for damages.

This book is sold subject to the conditions that it shall not,
by way of trade or otherwise, be lent, resold, hired out, or otherwise circulated
without the publisher's prior consent in any form or binding or cover other
than that in which it is published and without similar condition being
imposed on the subsequent purchaser.

Visit
www.salariya.com
for our online catalogue and
free fun stuff.

Chase Those Witches!

WRITTEN BY
ELIZABETH DALE

ILLUSTRATED BY
SIÂN ROBERTS

SCRIBBLERS

a SALARIYA *imprint*

This is Bernie. Isn't he the most adorable,
cuddly pet in the whole wide world?
He does wonderful tricks.
He croaks beautifully.
He comforts me when I'm feeling down...

He's always there for me.
Well, see for yourself... but he's rather shy.
So to make sure you don't scare him, turn the page
slowly and whisper 'HELLO LOVELY BERNIE' really softly.

Bernie's gone! Those mean witches have taken him.
Help me, please. Stop them!
Shake the book fast to make them crash.

Well done! One of them almost fell off.
But she still got away. They've all
escaped with my precious Bernie.
I have to rescue him. But how?
Look out! Duck before you get hit.

BRILLIANT!

I can follow those witches.
But how do I start flying? I've no idea.
Can you lift up the book, fast,
to get me into the air?

HOORAY! YOU DID IT! WHEeee!

Hooray! I'm at the South Pole! Uh-oh.
It's going to get really scary now.
I think you should put the book down.
I have to face the witches and rescue
Bernie, and it's absolutely

FREEEEEZING!

And I've got these friendly
penguins to help.
Whatever you do, don't...

NO!

YOU TURNED THE PAGE!

You opened the door to the ice cave.
You need to save us: tip the book up this side. Quick!

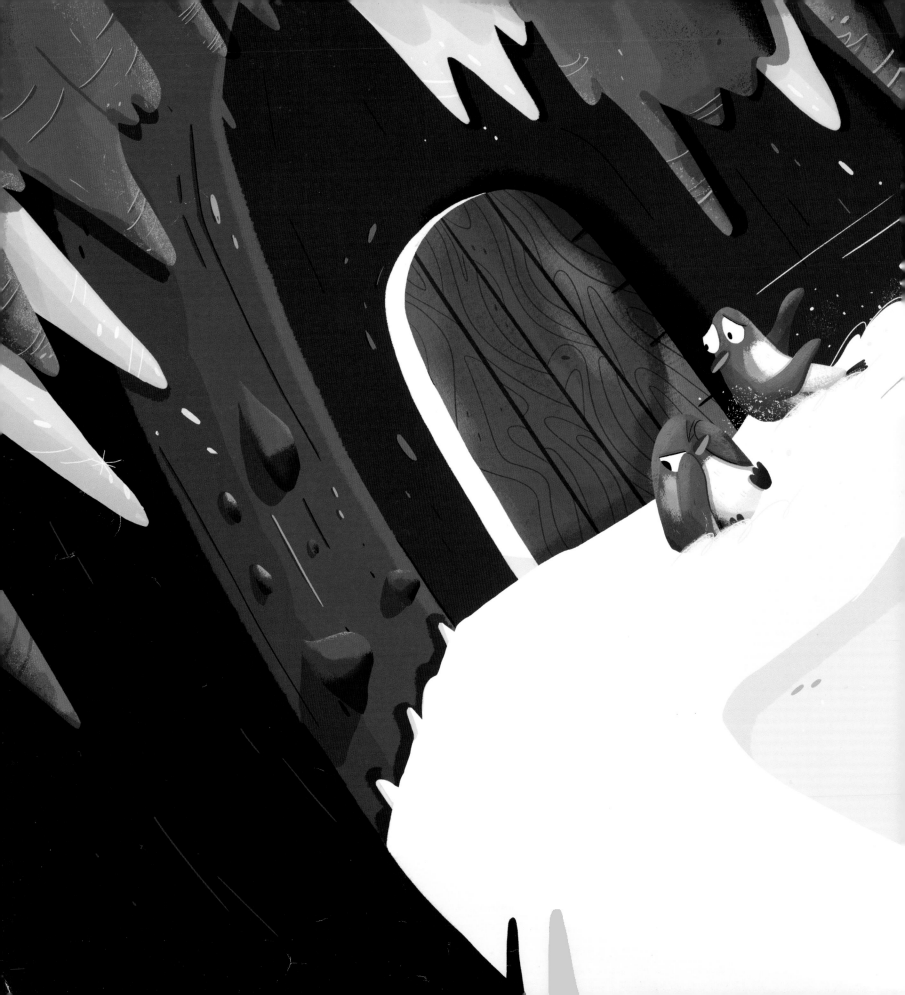

YOU TIPPED IT TOO FAR!

We're going to crash into the wall...
We've got to get around the bend.
Twirl the book around to help us.

FAST!

Uh-oh. Look, a monster! All that tipping and twirling has woken him up. He looks really grumpy. Quick, give him a stroke. Go on. Say **'LOVELY, SWEET MONSTER!'** Say it quickly, or he might...

ROAR!

Oh no, hide quickly! Behind a cushion, under a chair, anywhere. Don't make a sound...

Are you peeping?
Has the monster gone back
to sleep? Are you sure he's really asleep?
Let's all whisper **'MONSTER... COOO-EEE!'** to check.
No reply... Good.
Do you think the witches heard him and have
come looking?
I can't see them
anywhere...
Phew! I think we got
away with it. So, quick,
can you see Bernie?
Point to him if you can.
My poor little froggie must be so scared.

There he is. Bernie, oh, Bernie!
I've found you.
You're safe at last!
Aren't you just the most beautiful...

AAARGH!

Help, it's a witch attack! We've got to escape.
Look, up through that hole.
It's too narrow for them to fly through.
Turn the book upside down to tip us through it. Quick!

WATCH OUT!

The witches are coming down, too.
Penguins, hold on!
Reader, turn the book back the right way again.

HURRY!

Hooray! Well done, we're safe! And look, a skidoo. I've always wanted to ride a skidoo. We can get away before those witches escape the ice tunnel and come after us.

Oh no! It's stuck in the ice. Rub the ice with your fingers to melt it. Come on, you can do it...

Hooray, you did it!

WHEeee!

Uh-oh. What do we do now?

Silly penguins, are you CRAZY? I'm not riding on
your backs in that FREEEEZING water. No way!
Bernie's not keen either. Can anyone call out if you
can see anything that might help us get away?

Yes, great – a ship!
But oh no...

IT'S A PIRATE SHIP!

Whilst we hide, can you find
out if the pirates are on board?
Call out. You can do it. Cry
'IS ANYONE THERE?'
Go on!

Good, it looks as though the pirates are all ashore. Come on, penguins. Let's creep aboard. Brilliant, not a pirate in sight. But look, the witches are coming! We have to sail away fast! Penguins, unfurl the sails. Reader, blow us away. Please, blow harder!

COME ON, HARDER. YOU CAN DO IT!

HOORAY!
YOU DID IT!

We're sailing away. Those nasty witches can't get us. Let's pull funny faces at them and make rude noises. Go on!

Oh no. Look, the sea's freezing
around us. We're getting stuck!
Quick, the witches are coming.
They're going to get Bernie!
Bash their broomsticks to break them.
Then tap the side of the book to set us free.
HARD! KEEP GOING! COME ON...

PLEASE!

HOORAY!
YOU DID IT!

The witches can't fly after us and we're free! We're sailing away. Oh, this is lovely, it's getting warmer. I can even feel my toes again.

Thank you so much, you helped me save Bernie. All our troubles are over...

Mum will never even know we've been away. Everything is just as it was.

NEARLY...